AARON ZENZ

MONSTERS
Go Night-Night

ABRAMS APPLESEED • NEW YORK

The line art in *Monsters Go Night-Night* was created with
ink and brush and then digitally colored in Photoshop.

Cataloging-in-Publication Data has been applied for and
may be obtained from the Library of Congress.

ISBN: 978-1-4197-1653-9

Printed and bound in China
10 9 8 7 6 5 4 3 2 1

For bulk discount inquiries,
contact specialsales@abramsbooks.com.

ABRAMS
THE ART OF BOOKS SINCE 1949
115 West 18th Street
New York, NY 10011
www.abramsbooks.com

For Elijah, the Monster-Maker

MONSTERS
eat bedtime snacks.

Which snack do **MONSTERS** eat?

MONSTERS
eat
UMBRELLAS!

MONSTERS take baths.

What do **MONSTERS** take baths with?

MONSTERS
take baths with
CHOCOLATE PUDDING!

MONSTERS
wear pajamas.

What kind of pajamas do **MONSTERS** wear?

MONSTERS
wear
TOILET PAPER!

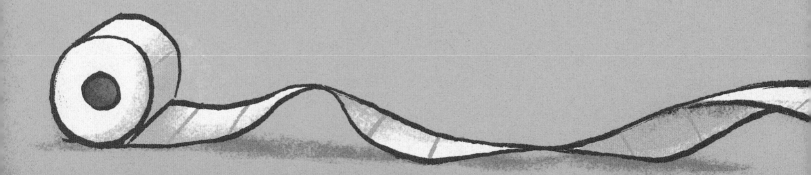

MONSTERS like to snuggle.

What do **MONSTERS**

snuggle with?

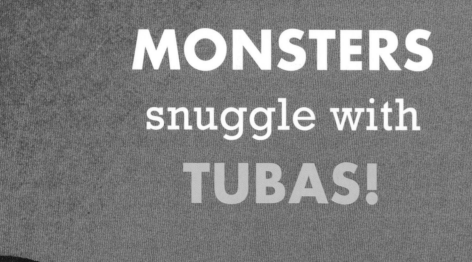

MONSTERS
snuggle with
TUBAS!

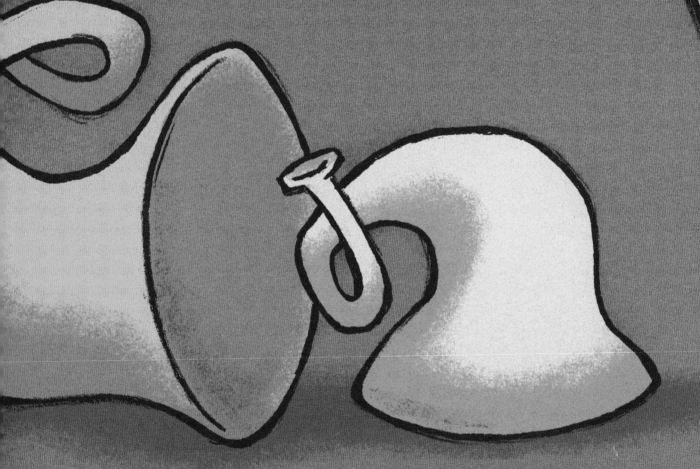

MONSTERS
clean their teeth.

How do **MONSTERS**
clean their teeth?

MONSTERS
clean their
teeth with an
OCTOPUS!

MONSTERS
need to go potty.

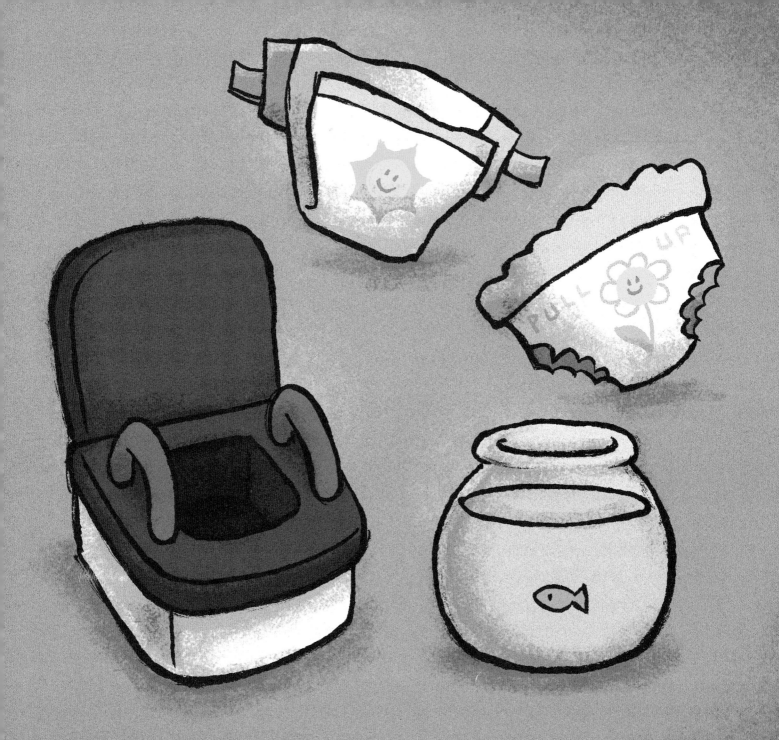

Where do **MONSTERS** go?

MONSTERS

go in the

TOILET!

(Whew! It's a good thing
MONSTERS know where to go.)

MONSTERS love
night-night kisses.

Whom do **MONSTERS**
love to kiss?

Night-
night,
Mommy.

Night-
night,
Daddy.

Night-night, Baby.

And *night*-night, **PIZZA!**